TURBO

THE DUEL

MITSUBISHI ECLIPSE

Nathan Sacks

MINNEAPOLIS

Darby Creek
A division of Lerner Publishing Group, Inc.
241 First Avenue North
Minneapolis, MN 55401 U.S.A.

Website address: www.lernerbooks.com

The images in this book are used with the permisison of:
Cover and interior photograph © Road & Track Magazine/Jeff Allen/ Transtock/CORBIS.

Main body text set in Janson Text LT Std 12/17.
Typeface provided by Linotype AG.

Library of Congress Cataloging-in-Publication Data

Sacks, Nathan.
     The duel : Mitsubishi Eclipse / by Nathan Sacks.
          pages   cm. — (Turbocharged)
     ISBN 978-1-4677-1243-9 (lib. bdg. : alk. paper)
     ISBN 978-1-4677-1669-7 (eBook)
     [1. Mitsubishi Lancer automobile—Fiction. 2. Automobiles—Fiction.
3. Muscle cars—Fiction.] I. Title.
     PZ7.S1224Du 2013
     [Fic]—dc23   2013008089

Manufactured in the United States of America
1 – BP – 7/15/13

FOR MY BROTHERS,
JEREMY AND AARON

PROLOGUE

In Connor, Alaska, the longest stretch of road goes only a mile. If you walked across Main Street, it would take about an hour to get from one end to the other. You would expect that in a town as small as Connor, everyone walked everywhere. But some people preferred to drive.

Since there was nowhere to go exploring, teenagers raced one another at night, when Main Street was most empty.

Parents were constantly worried. The Connor police watched Main Street closely.

But they couldn't stop the kids all the time. As soon as the police left, the teens would set up another race and burn two new sets of tracks into the road.

Teenagers in Connor loved cars, but they loved one thing even more: defying authority. They rebelled against parents, police, or teachers—anyone who believed in the rules. But one cold night eight years ago challenged that spirit of rebellion.

A race was scheduled between two kids from Connor High. Though Freddie Franklin and Cliff Genie both did well in school and in sports, they were in trouble constantly. The police knew them by their first names. Freddie and Cliff were old enough to drive, despite restricted licenses because of speeding violations.

Freddie and Cliff were also known for being friendly to everyone, even when they caused trouble. They just needed more excitement in their lives, the locals said.

Freddie was lean and muscular. He was maybe the best high school football player in

Alaska. Everyone assumed he had a shot at the NFL. He was that talented. And yet, he never bragged about his skills. Besides, they weren't his main focus. Cars were.

Cliff also played football, but he was rougher than his friend. He did less well in school and spent more time goofing off in class. But people liked him too.

The race that night was a chicky run. Instead of racing side by side, cars started on opposite sides of the street. Both cars would drive straight at the other as fast as possible. Whoever swerved first to avoid the crash lost. The loser was called the chicken.

On the west side of Main Street, where the road's asphalt turned into dirt and gravel, Cliff sat in a gray Oldsmobile. His hands were tight on the wheel. He revved his suped-up engine. Cliff was impatient for the race to start. He waved at fellow students to get out of his way, honking his horn as he moved to the starting line.

Cliff could see a tiny outline of his best friend's car a mile away. He could also see the

Spiff Tube tire repair shop, where his father Del had always worked. Spiff Tube was the biggest business in town. The owner was a local millionaire named Edmond Tremonte.

Everyone in town knew Tremonte, but not very well. Because he was so rich, Tremonte didn't have a lot in common with small-town folks. He never had a good relationship with Del, even though Cliff's father was the best mechanic at Spiff Tube. The store was in a prime spot: the only intersection in the middle of Main Street, halfway between where Cliff and Freddie were idling.

Cliff heard Freddie honk his horn. It roared *bwaaamp!* in a friendly fashion. Cliff honked back to his friend and smiled. *Bwaaamp!* This would be an epic race.

Cliff thought about his younger sister, Patty, and his younger brother, Ken. He wanted to show them this part of his life. He wanted to show them why driving was so important, especially in a tiny town with nothing to do.

A flag girl stepped in front of Cliff's car

and waved a bandana. It was time for the chicky run to start.

Cliff suddenly felt scared. Had he checked everything? The flag girl started counting down.

"3!"

Cliff gripped his steering wheel tight again.

"2!"

The rest of the crowd joined in. Cliff eased on the clutch and went into first gear.

"1!"

Cliff gunned the accelerator. Smoke blew behind him as he revved into second gear, then third. In the next minute, anything could happen. Cliff felt weightless, as if he were flying through the air in a rocket.

Freddie's car became larger in his windshield. They were within a half mile of each other. Neither Cliff nor Freddie slowed a bit. They kept going faster, and getting closer and closer to each other.

Cliff briefly wondered what every driver wonders during a chicky run: *What happens if neither of us brake? What happens if no one blinks?*

They were within two hundred feet of each other, then one hundred, going faster. Either one of them swerved, or this was it.

Maybe it's okay to be a chicken, Cliff thought, as he sped past 100 MPH.

There was a loud screech. Cliff opened his eyes to see Freddie spinning off the road. Freddie's car had hit a small patch of ice. It whirled madly two or three times before crashing bumper first into the closest building: the Spiff Tube garage. It blew through the garage door and knocked over the wall on the other side. Debris and sparks were everywhere. The clanging metal and broken glass were the worst sounds Cliff had ever heard.

Cliff slammed on the brakes and sped out from the road into an open field. As soon as the car came to rest, Cliff got out of it and raced toward his friend. On the bitter Alaska night, the last thing he noticed was the cold.

The scene was worse than he feared. Freddie's car had collided with another car idling in the garage. The mixture of high pressure, oil, and sparks had started a fire that was spreading through the shop. Cliff found Freddie's body, slumped over the broken passenger window, badly injured. The fire made it too hot to get near the car.

"Cliff!" Freddie cried desperately.

Avoiding the car's hot metal, Cliff lifted Freddie over his arms and pulled him through the hole in the garage wall. The fire was swallowing everything around them. Car paint peeled, floors cracked, and tanks of gas exploded as Cliff carried Freddie to safety.

Cliff laid his friend carefully in the street. He heard sirens. The police and fire department were coming to the scene.

Within seconds, emergency providers were loading Freddie Franklin onto a stretcher and then into an ambulance vehicle. As the EMTs closed the back doors, Cliff could hear them talking about burns and Freddie's breathing.

Cliff tried to keep his thoughts straight as he walked back toward his car.

The rest of the town was descending on

the scene. Something had happened to the football star. Freddie was the town's best hope in decades, an athlete so good he was going to put Connor on the map. Cliff noticed the adults looking at him with blame in their eyes.

Cliff thought about his brother and sister again. Pride and love were replaced with deep shame. Then he thought about his father and mother. How could he do this to his dad's employer?

Minutes earlier, Cliff Genie had been a rebellious free spirit. But he hung his head as the police took his vehicle and put him in handcuffs.

The town was not going to be the same after that. But it wasn't finished changing, either.

CHAPTER ONE

After the incident, police in Connor cracked
down on street racing. Main Street became a
ghost street. The only drivers you'd see were
travelers, not locals. Teenagers stayed at home
or hung out in school.

The explosion at Spiff Tube had left a
broken mess. Edmond Tremonte, who owned
many other Spiff Tube stores around Alaska
and Canada, demolished what was left. With
the insurance payout, he had plenty of money
to build the store back from scratch. In the
next year, Tremonte built an improved Spiff

Tube at the same location. The new store would be the next chapter in his life, he thought. He had a number of ideas to expand business. But with the cost of the upgrades, Tremonte had to fire someone.

Cliff Genie's father, Del Genie, was the first victim. Everyone knew Del was the best mechanic in Connor. Tremonte depended on Del's knowledge and love of cars to attract business. But Edmond could no longer afford his oldest employees. He fired Del as soon as his insurance came in. The next day, he hired a cheap batch of high school workers. Some people suspected that Edmond fired Del out of revenge. Edmond denied it, but even his money could not silence the local gossip.

A few months after Del lost his job, he learned he had stomach cancer. His friends suggested that being fired had broken his spirit. The Genie family had trouble paying Del's medical bills.

One day, Ellen Genie traveled to Edmond Tremonte's townhouse to ask for help. She wasn't begging. She was demanding what she knew the family deserved.

"Your son trashed my store, and you want charity from *me*?" Edmond asked from his front porch.

"My husband ran that place for thirty-four years while you flew around pitching new stores in Canada."

"Get off my porch," Edmond scowled and slammed the front door in her face.

Freddie disappeared after leaving the hospital. Rumor was that horrible burns still covered his body. Some had heard that he had lost use of one leg. One thing was clear: Freddie Franklin was out of football for good. He became homeschooled. Then he moved away. Freddie never said goodbye, not even to Cliff.

Cliff Genie felt so guilty over what happened to Freddie, he could barely concentrate in school. Cliff's grades started to suffer. He started to get in fights. As he watched his life come apart, Cliff decided he was done with Connor. Early one night, he went to his father's sickbed.

"Pop, I keep thinking about what happened to you, to our family, to Freddie . . ."

"Speed to the point, son. I have cancer." When things got dark, Del always tried to be funny. Cliff, holding back tears, could not laugh.

"I want to leave, pop. Everyone in town looks at me like I killed someone. My friends walk away when they see me coming."

"Cliff, you made a mistake. But you saved someone. I was at that store too long, and besides, the boss is rotten."

Cliff held his father's hand. Del could barely grip back.

"I understand if it is too hard being here," Del said. "But I want you to promise two things for me. First, promise that you will come back if your family needs you."

"I'll try," Cliff replied.

"No trying. Promise me."

"So I promise. What's the other thing?"

Del told his son the other thing, and Cliff sat by Del's side as he fell asleep. Then Cliff packed some clothes, got into his Oldsmobile, and left town.

✳ ✳ ✳

Del died in his bed a week later. Ken and Patty were at his side. No one could get hold of Cliff.

"I could never forgive Cliff for not being here," Ellen told herself at Del's funeral. Ken and Patty were both with her, as was the rest of Connor. "How could my son stay away on this day?"

Ken, eight years old, adjusted his large glasses and tried to come up with an answer. He knew he still loved his brother. It hurt to see his mother say these things.

The local reverend began a eulogy. "We lay to rest Del Genie, father of three, husband of the beautiful Ellen, and a genius with cars . . ."

Some people laughed. But one person laughed harder. It was fake, mocking laughter.

"Genius, hah!" The voice came from

the back of the procession. It was Edmond Tremonte, leaning on another man's grave. He pointed his finger at the people of Connor.

"Poor Del! Poor Del!" Tremonte said. He moved through the crowd to speak directly to Del's coffin. "As if he never caused anyone any grief. What about what your son did to my store?"

He turned to the crowd again. "Poor Edmond, is what you *all* should be saying! Poor me!"

"Be quiet, Tremonte," a local said. "This is a man's funeral!"

Tremonte interrupted him. "Without my store, what would Del Genie be? My money gave him his craft. My money fixed your cars."

There were more shouts: "We don't want you in our town no more, Tremonte!"

"Wait, wait!" Tremonte cried.

"All right, that's it!" A police officer attending the funeral grabbed Tremonte. The officer pushed him against a tree and handcuffed him. Some people clapped as Edmond Tremonte was led into a police car.

The funeral continued without interruption. But there was a different feeling now. Ken kept thinking about what his mother said. *I'll never forgive Cliff.* The words haunted Ken like the ghost of his father.

After that, no one saw Edmond Tremonte. Sometimes, cars on Main Street noticed an outline in a Spiff Tube window—in Edmond Tremonte's office. It looked like the shape of a man in jail, pressed against the bars. Desperate to plot some kind of insane revenge on the people who put him there.

CHAPTER TWO

"Ken Genie, it's time to wake up!"

His sister's voice brought him out of a deep sleep. Ken was dreaming about cars. He had been cruising on an endless freeway, the sun warming his face. As Ken put on his glasses, the dream faded away. Time for school.

Patty Genie stood at the foot of Ken's bed and grabbed his covers. She had graduated from high school a year ago but had stayed to help the family. She was a waitress in Farber, the next big town over. She helped pay the Genie family bills. Patty was a short woman with a bright face. But underneath her brightness, she was very sarcastic. Everyone who saw her said she looked (and sounded) like her mother.

Ken's mom was waiting for him in the kitchen. Ellen was like her daughter, except she worried a lot more. She offered her son a bowl of cereal and a hard-boiled egg.

"You have to take the bus today," she said to Ken as he ate in big gulps.

He dreaded those words. "But Mom—"

"No walking outside," she replied firmly. In Connor, sometimes it was too cold to walk. Ken had no license, and his family had no car. This meant that he had to take the school bus.

"I turned sixteen. Why don't you let me get my license?"

Ellen Genie shook her head. "You remember your brother. Take the bus and be safe."

Patty walked into the kitchen then and handed a bag lunch to her little brother.

"Out!" the female Genies of the house both yelled. The school bus was just passing by. Ken ran through the cold toward it.

*   *   *

You remember your brother. Ken thought about those words as he sat on the bus. He looked out through his glasses at another Alaska sunrise. Cliff Genie had been gone for almost eight years. Ken missed him more than words could say.

Ken knew he had a lot in common with his brother. First and foremost, they loved cars. In the past eight years, Ken had become the biggest gearhead in town. When he was in sixth grade, he read all the books in school about cars. After devouring everything there, he moved on to his local library. Eight years later, you could find Ken Genie on the computer after school, Googling car photos or making notes about custom specs.

Ken's mother had a different opinion about cars. She had grown up in New York City and hated driving. Since the Spiff Tube crash, she was convinced that cars were too dangerous. She didn't let Patty get a license until Patty was eighteen. Ken was sixteen, and he still took the bus with all the younger kids. To Ken, being this age and having no car was torture.

Luckily, the ride was short. Ken exited the bus behind a row of freshmen. He noticed his friend Benno Lester standing outside school.

While Ken was just a car nerd, Benno was a full-on nerd-nerd. He loved anything related to science fiction. He was a great artist with an untamed imagination. While other kids played sports or hung out, Ken and Benno designed blueprints for futuristic cars and other vehicles. Benno would show a design for atomic-powered flying cars, and Ken would make sure the hood was large enough to fit an atomic engine. Basically, Benno was the idea man, and Ken helped those ideas make sense.

Unfortunately, they did not have many other friends at school. With only five hundred kids, everyone at Connor High knew one another. Most people recognized Ken and stayed away. He was known as the kid whose brother ditched town. Ken was not as athletic as his brother, and his thick glasses didn't help.

But he had at least one good friend in Benno. Together, they walked through the school doors.

"I just came up with something crazy," Benno said. "A hovertank!"

It didn't take an engineer to realize that there was no way a hovering tank would work in real life. "We'll talk after first period," Ken responded.

First period meant industrial technology class. I-Tech was Ken's favorite. Ms. Torres, the teacher, was another major gearhead, and her teaching was always fun. Ms. Torres also pulled double duty as the school's driving instructor. Before letting students behind the wheel, she would make them open the hood and name everything inside, from the battery to the carburetor. Ken would have aced the test, if his mom ever let him take the class.

Ms. Torres and Ken would talk about their favorite imports and models between periods.

During I-Tech, however, she was all business. That day she was teaching electricity.

"Can anyone tell me about Ohm's law?" she asked the class.

Ken raised his hand.

"V = IR," he said. "It measures the difference between voltage and current. Er, something like that."

Voices behind Ken murmured "nerd," hiding their laughter.

One student who didn't laugh was Stacey Grenzer. She was Ken's lab partner. While Ken loved cars more than anything, he liked Stacey a lot too. She had short brown hair and dark eyes that bugged out a bit when she was thinking hard. Ken tried not to stare at her in class, but sometimes it was tough.

After the class bell, Ken walked up to Ms. Torres's desk, where she sat grading papers.

"Ken, did you see the latest *Car & Driver* magazine?" she asked. "I could give you my copy during study hall."

"That's fine. I already read it at the library."

"What's up?"

"Ms. Torres, my mom still won't let me drive. I still know more about how to drive and fix cars than anyone I know . . ."

"You have the knack, Ken. But students can't take a driving course until a parent gives permission. Otherwise, you have to wait until you're eighteen. That's state law."

"But it's not fair!" Ken explained. "She's scared because of my brother. I was born to drive, just like him, and my mom knows it too."

"Maybe you were," Ms. Torres said. "But imagine if you had someone you cared about. Imagine if they almost died in a car crash. Can you understand why she would be worried?"

Ken did understand, but he didn't want to admit it. "Can't you let me take a little drive, just to feel what it's like?"

"Let me try to help," Ms. Torres offered. "Maybe in the next few days the three of us can have a conversation."

"Really?" The possibility was enough to excite Ken.

"Let's talk later. Go get to class," Ms.

Torres ordered.

⁕ ⁕ ⁕

It was warmer out when school ended. Ken skipped the bus and walked home with Benno. Snow fell gently around them.

"I hear you keep staring at Stacey, you freak," Benno teased.

"Shut up, Benno." If it wasn't already freezing outside, Ken's cheeks would have turned red.

"She thinks you're smart, Ken," Benno continued. "I heard her say it in the lunchroom. You should ask her out or something."

"And go where?" Ken asked. They were nearing his block. "Anyway, I can't drive. What would she want with me?"

"Maybe she hit her head on a rock or something. Hey, Ken, your family doesn't have a car, right?"

"That's right."

"Then what's in your driveway?"

There was a car in the driveway of the house ahead. A nice car. And on the passenger side, there was a sign:

FOR KENNETH GENIE ON THE OCCASION OF HIS 16TH BIRTHDAY

"For you?" Benno asked.

For *me?* Ken was speechless.

CHAPTER THREE

Ken recognized the bright-red car in his driveway. It was curved and sleek, almost like a missile.

"It's a Mitsubishi Eclipse," he said.

"A what?"

"It's a Japanese sport compact. They started making these in the eighties. Super powerful, super fast. Two-liter engine . . . Looks like one of the turbo models . . ."

"What does that mean? Why is it in your driveway?"

"It must be a mistake. This looks like a

brand-new car, but it must be like fifteen years old."

Benno and Ken circled around the car, staring through the windows. Ken opened the driver's seat door. It was unlocked.

"Benno, take a look at the odometer!"

"Sure!" Benno peeked inside the vehicle. "Uh, what is that?"

"The thing that says how many miles you've driven. There's about a thousand miles on this fifteen-year-old car."

"Are you serious?" Benno asked.

"Yup."

"So it is brand-new. Kinda."

"Yup, and the keys are right here. And the car's registration."

Ken popped the car's hood, then moved to look underneath. "This engine's like nothing I've ever seen," he said. "Totally customized. The horsepower on this thing's got to be incredible."

"Did your mom get this?" Benno asked.

"No way. She hates cars. And she couldn't afford it. Who could buy a custom job like this?"

"Someone like Edmond Tremonte," Benno said.

Ken didn't respond. He remembered Tremonte's actions at his father's funeral. A gift from that guy seemed unlikely.

Ken looked at the registration papers. His name was at the top. "So this is my car," he said, "and I don't have a license!"

"What will your mom think?" Benno asked.

Ken really, really had no idea.

✳ ✳ ✳

Ken spent the rest of the afternoon in his room, trying to do homework. Mostly, he stared at the car outside his window. He read the registration papers again. They were still in his name. Was this even legal?

Ken's neighbors began to notice the car too. Some stopped in the street to stare at it.

Who would leave a teenage kid a car like this? Ken tried to think, but no explanation made any sense. Some kids at school had nice cars but nothing at this level. There was a mystery here, and it needed solving.

* * *

Ellen Genie came home later that night and went into Ken's room. She was just as confused as he was.

"Whose car is this?" she asked. There were still neighbors outside.

"It's in my name, Mom," he said, showing her the paperwork. "For some reason, it belongs to me."

Ellen sat down on Ken's bed. "No, it doesn't. It's a mistake, and we will get rid of it."

"But, Mom!" Ken knew an argument was coming.

"No license and no insurance means no car. Give me the keys."

"But it's in my name! You can't just take something like this and throw it away!"

"I will sell it tomorrow if I have to. Wherever it came from, it goes back. Do you understand?"

"No, I don't!"

"Do you want to end up like your brother? You're so much like him, Ken. The way you look at cars—I know you feel something deep with them. Just like Cliff."

Ken was furious. "So I can't drive a car because I would like it too much," he spat. "Thanks, Mom."

"I'm selling it," she repeated. "If you want to help, go to the Spiff Tube tonight and buy us a weatherproof car cover. We should protect it from the snow." She looked out the window. "And I don't like how the neighbors are acting around this car."

At the Spiff Tube, Ken walked into the front office. Around him were the sounds of clattering machinery and whirring tools. The person at the counter was a high school kid playing *Angry Birds*. It took the kid a while to realize he had a customer.

"Uh, can I help you?" he asked.

"I need a weatherproof tarp cover. For a car."

"You looking for a special size, or . . ."

"I can pick it myself," Ken interrupted. "Just point me to where they are."

"Er, let me ask my manager." The kid pressed a bell on his desk and waited for the manager to come out of his office. Eventually, Edmond Tremonte opened his office door.

Tremonte had changed over the past eight years. After Del Genie's funeral, Tremonte had finally accepted that the town didn't like him. He decided to hate it back.

Tremonte recognized Ken. His lips curled into something that almost looked like a smile. "Ken Genie! How are you, son?"

"Okay," Ken said. "I just want a weatherproof cover."

"A cover? Does the Genie family have a new car?"

Ken sensed that he should keep quiet. "Oh, you know. Just in case we need it."

Tremonte could tell the boy was lying, but he went into the back of the store and brought out a few different boxes. Ken picked the correct size.

"Please, Ken, take this for free. For your family." Tremonte was in salesman mode.

"No thanks. I'd prefer to pay," Ken said, holding out his money.

Tremonte chuckled and opened the cash register. "A strong will. Like your father."

Ken said nothing, took his change, and left. He figured the less of Edmond Tremonte in his life, the better.

Tremonte was suspicious all that night. *Why buy a car cover without a car?* After work, he visited the Genies' house and noticed something large in the driveway. A thick tarp covered something that was shaped a lot like a car. He looked under it.

I know this car, Edmond Tremonte thought. *It belongs to me!*

After returning to Spiff Tube, he locked himself in his office and began to think.

CHAPTER FOUR

No one had to wake Ken for school the next day. He hadn't slept all night. He kept staring at the driveway. Silently, he prayed the Eclipse would still be there when he got home from school. He would do anything to keep this car.

Ken moved through school that day like a ghost. Even Benno had trouble getting him to speak.

"Ken, everyone knows about the car."

They were sitting together at a lunch table.

"My mom is getting rid of it."

"When?"

"Probably today." Ken looked sadly into his disgusting school lunch. He didn't notice that Stacey had walked to their table.

"Do you mind if I sit here?" she asked.

"Heck yes!" said Benno. "I mean no! No, we don't mind, right Ken?"

Ken was in no mood. Being around Stacey made him feel weak. He was bad at talking, but he was really bad at talking to girls.

Benno grinned. "It looks like I have, uh, things to do," he said. He packed what remained of his lunch and walked away.

"So everyone at school is talking about a slick new car in your driveway..." Stacey began.

"It's a Mitsubishi Eclipse. They're, uh, pretty nice cars and pretty fast."

"How fast can they go?" she asked, genuinely curious.

"Pretty fast. Really, really fast." Ken stared into his mashed potatoes, avoiding her gaze. He was afraid of saying something too nerdy.

"Where did it come from?"

"I don't know. But my mom is selling it

today, so it doesn't even matter."

"Sad," she responded. "It sounds like a great car. Don't you still want to find out where it's from?"

Ken finally looked into her face. She looked right back at him. It nearly stopped his heart. "Maybe I should."

"Have you ever skipped school before?" Stacey asked.

"My brother did it a lot before he left. My mom would kill me."

"So would my mom, but I have a free period. Let's get out of here."

"But the car might be gone!" Ken tried to argue, but Stacey did not seem to care.

They ducked out the doors and into the school parking lot.

Ken rode in the passenger side of Stacey's car. Her ride was creaky, old, and rusty, but at least she had one.

Stacey asked him questions as she drove.

"You mentioned your brother before. Can you tell me more about him?"

Ken shrugged and adjusted his glasses. "He's gone. There's not much else to it."

"I'm sorry," she said.

He tried to explain. "Sometimes I say things to people, and they sound rude, but I don't mean it that way. Cliff was a cool brother, and I liked him a lot. This whole town hates him, though. It's why they hate me too."

Stacey pulled up to the curb in front of the Genie house. The Eclipse was still in the driveway, still covered.

"It's there!" Stacey pointed out.

Ken turned to his new friend. "Wanna look inside?"

"Would I?"

Together, they exited the vehicle and approached the Eclipse. Ken lifted up the tarp and beckoned to Stacey. "Come on in."

41

They spent the next hour underneath a heavy blue tarp. It was the happiest hour of Ken's life. He told her as much as he had ever told anyone about cars. He described the Eclipse's turbocharged engine, its powerful torque, and its smooth steering. He told her his plans for modifying the engine, making it even faster. Then he talked about his mom and her fear of cars. Stacey was a good listener.

"So I can sit in the car as much as I want, but I can't drive it," he explained.

"Totally unfair," Stacey agreed. "But what if your mom didn't know?"

"What does that mean?"

"Do you know where the keys are?"

"I . . . think I do." He remembered the chain with the house keys, right by the door.

The spirit of rebellion was alive in Ken at that moment. Unfortunately, the trip never happened. Ellen had just arrived. Ken still had the keys when he came outside.

"Ken Genie, get away from that car!" Ellen yelled. Stacey noticed her shouting and sheepishly stepped out of the Eclipse.

"Mom, this is my friend Stacey..." Ken was still holding the car keys.

"Stacey, please go home. And *you*, go to your room and don't come out."

"This is my car, Mom," Ken said. "The paperwork is in my name, so it's still mine!"

"Do I have to remind you of your brother again?"

Ken finally had enough. "Who cares about my brother? Why do you have to measure him against me? If you hate him so much, and I'm just like my brother, why do you even care?"

"Ken, you don't under..."

"One interesting thing happens in this boring town, and you ruin it! Just like Cliff!"

Ken made a split-second decision. He started running. He couldn't face Stacey and his mother. They yelled at him to come back as he fled down the street. He ran to the end of his block, then kept running.

In the end, Ken ran as far as a frozen lake on the edge of town. For the next few hours, he sat in the middle of the lake and looked at the stars. He imagined being a Formula One racer, hitting incredible speeds while fans screamed. Then he dreamed of being a stunt driver in Hollywood. Then he dreamed of owning his own car shop or designing models for companies like Mitsubishi. For a few hours, he dreamed of everything except being a sixteen-year-old kid in a small town in Alaska.

Eventually it became too cold, and Ken had to go back. He trudged to the Genie house, where the Eclipse was still in the driveway.

He walked through the door into his house, expecting another lecture from his mother. Instead, he found Ellen, Patty, and Stacey, laughing around the dinner table. Ken smelled delicious home-cooked food.

Patty called to him. "Brother? Did I hear a brother come in? Come sit and have a meal with us, brother."

Ken walked into the kitchen. There was an extra chair and a plate at the table waiting.

"I was just talking to your friend Stacey," explained Ellen. "I called her mother to invite her for supper. Is that okay?"

Ken had to suppress a smile. "All right," he tried to say casually. After dreaming of better things for hours, his family brought him back to earth. He put away his anger and joined the conversation.

Stacey spoke. "So we were talking about our favorite car movies. What's your favorite?"

The answer for Ken was easy. "*Gone in 60 Seconds*, no question."

"I always liked the *Knight Rider* show, with David Hasselhoff," said Patty.

"If talking cars count, my favorite is *Herbie the Love Bug*," Ellen said. Then she became serious. "Ken, I think you were a bit hard on me earlier. But maybe you were a little right too. We all need to listen to each other more. So I didn't sell the car today. I've given some thought . . ."

Suddenly, there was a sharp knock on the door. Everyone looked around the table. No one was expecting company.

"I'll get that," Ellen said.

While Ellen was gone, Patty said, "So, are you two friends, or what?"

Ken was red. He looked at Stacey, and she laughed. At the same time, Ellen opened the front door to greet the visitor. A voice from outside carried into the kitchen.

"Hello, I'm Edmond Tremonte," the voice said. "You may remember me. May I please come in?"

CHAPTER FIVE

Edmond Tremonte stood in the Genie
kitchen, his hat in his hand. Dinner was put on
hold.

Ellen had not forgotten the way Tremonte
had treated her family. And no one in town
forgot the pathetic display at Del's funeral.
The atmosphere inside was as tense as the cold
outside.

Edmond spoke to Ken. "And how is the
weather cover holding up?"

"Fine," said Ken.

"At Spiff Tube, we only buy the highest

quality. That's a slogan I just came up with. Did you like my new shop?"

Ken said nothing.

"Who are you?" Tremonte asked Stacey.

Before she could respond, Ellen interrupted. "Do you want something? You're interrupting dinner with my family. In Mom's house, that's a bad, bad idea."

"Er . . ." Tremonte began. "I don't want to spoil your meal, so let's speak quickly. It occurred to me, after young Ken was at my store, that the Genies had no car. It also occurred to me, just yesterday, that now you must."

"So . . ." Ellen replied, her arms crossed.

"And I think you accidentally have a car that belongs to me."

"Oh, do I?" Ellen said.

"The vehicle outside was a gift to me from a beloved customer. I lost it, or someone stole it from me."

"Who stole it?"

"Does it matter?"

"Is there proof? A police report?"

"I believe the thief stole that too . . ."

"The car doesn't belong to you. It's my son's."

Ken was thrilled hearing his mother say those words.

"From what I understand, your son is no driver. But who can blame you for being overprotective, since losing your oldest?"

Ellen gritted her teeth. "You treated my husband like trash when he was alive. Then you ruined his funeral. You want my son's car? Guess what? You can't have it."

"Of course I don't want to just take it." He brought a checkbook from his coat pocket. "I'm willing to pay whatever price you need to get it back. Would you sell it for $30,000? $40,000? I can go as high as $50,000."

"You can't have it."

"Imagine a big, big pile of money. All for a car you never saw before yesterday."

"We do fine with money now, thank you." Ellen had never had a chance to truly tell Tremonte off. Del would have been proud. She turned to Ken. "What do you think, Ken? Do you want to sell it to this guy?"

Money never beats cars. "Never," he said.

Edmond Tremonte frowned. "Look. You either give me this car, or I will take it from you. Now or later."

"Get out of my house or I call the police," Ellen finally said.

"Already called them," said Patty.

Tremonte was indignant. "You want to bring in the law? Try it."

Two cops arrived minutes later.

* * *

"Let me guess: Edmond Tremonte, our worst resident, is at it again," said one cop, as they led Tremonte out the door.

"This town is sick of your antics, Edmond," said the other cop. "I don't know why you don't move to Canada."

"Officers!" Tremonte protested. "The car belongs to me! I can prove it!"

"Maybe, but you can't stay here."

"How dare you!" Tremonte cried. "How

dare you call this justice!" He turned to Ellen. "Ellen Genie, mark my words. If you do not return what is rightfully mine, this town will suffer!"

"Yeah, yeah, suffer," said the other cop. "Ma'am, would you like to press charges?"

"Yes," Ellen said. Ken felt pride like nothing else for his mother. He looked at Stacey. She seemed to be amazed too.

By the time he was led to the police car, Tremonte was screaming. "This is it, Genies!" he yelled. "I'll bail myself out, and then I'm coming for this car!"

Stacey left the house not long after. She thanked the Genies for the food and said goodbye to Ken on the front stoop.

"See you in first period," she said.

It was an exciting night.

Later, Ken and his mother sat next to each other on the living room couch, watching TV.

"Mom, that was so awesome," Ken said.

"You really showed that guy something."

But Ellen seemed to be worried. "Ken, just out of curiosity, how would you stop someone from stealing a car?"

"Block the steering wheel, take off a tire, remove the battery, unplug the transmission . . . why?"

"How about we go out and play with the car a little bit? Maybe take out the transmission."

"Do you really think he would try?"

"He was your dad's boss and a sneaky jerk. So he might try."

Together, they went outside.

"Here's what we do," Ken explained. He opened the Eclipse's hood and disconnected the negative battery cable. Then he disconnected the throttle linkage from the carburetor. Then he put a jack underneath the car and started disconnecting all the wiring and draining the transmission fluid.

"Can you put this back together?" Ellen asked.

"Oh yeah," Ken said. "Don't worry, Mom."

"Ken, you know how I say you're so much like your brother?"

"Yeah?" Ken shouted as he worked underneath the hood of the car.

"Maybe I was wrong. You're more like your father. He loved getting underneath cars, taking them apart, pulling them together."

"It's just who I am. It's what I want to do with my life." Ken moved from under the car. "Done."

They walked back inside. For the rest of the night, Ken eagerly told his mother more about his dreams, and she listened, just as eagerly.

❊ ❊ ❊

Edmond Tremonte came back later that night. Anyone with that amount of money never spends too long in jail. While the Genie family slept, Tremonte crept to the Eclipse and took out a box of tools. He tried to hotwire the car to start, but the transmission was blocked. It made terrible noises that the neighbors immediately heard. Realizing he'd been outsmarted, Tremonte fled once more into the night.

CHAPTER SIX

No one saw much of Tremonte after that.
But they definitely heard something at the
Spiff Tube. Business suddenly shut down.
The boss fired everyone and retreated into his
workshop. For the next few days, citizens of
Connor could hear loud noises and bangs from
inside the Spiff Tube.

"What's he building in there?" locals asked
one another.

Tremonte put black paint over the
windows so no one could see inside. Welding
noises seemed to last all day and all night.

Still, people said, at least Tremonte was keeping to himself. He didn't come out of that store for the next five days.

Soon it was Monday again, the start of a new school week. Things were working for the Genie family, for once. Ken still had no license, but his mom seemed more open to the idea. He also had a new friend in Stacey. He still couldn't believe she had stayed for dinner that one night.

But he wasn't afraid to look her in the eyes anymore.

While other students slept at their desks, Ken was eager to listen to Ms. Torres. She wrote on a whiteboard, *BASIC CIRCUITRY DESIGN*. Ken knew some of this but listened anyway. Couldn't hurt to review.

After class, Ken promised to meet with Stacey at lunch. Then he went to talk to Ms. Torres.

"I know what you're going to ask me," she

said. "You want me to talk to your mother."

"Is that okay?"

"How about I come home with you after school?"

For Ken, any time would have worked perfectly.

* * *

Ellen Genie was home when they arrived. Ken quickly introduced his mother to Ms. Torres. They seemed to get along and even made some small talk. At least it sounded like small talk. Ken wasn't really listening.

Eventually, the conversation changed to cars. Ms. Torres sat on a chair in the family living room. Ken and Ellen sat together on their couch.

"I wanted you to know, you have one heck of a bright son," Ms. Torres said.

"I see his report card," Ellen replied with suspicion.

"I also teach the driver's education program at the school. Ken is really interested, you know."

"I know. And I bet Ken told you about my . . . problems with cars."

"You're scared of people being hurt in them." Ms. Torres was trying to be direct as possible.

"It's not like I've never been right."

"Ken has a special love for cars," Ms. Torres continued. "He has a special gift for them too."

"So did his father," Ellen replied. "But I hate cars, and I hate driving."

"Why?"

"How many reasons do you want? They ruin the environment. They lead to crashes and deaths. They take up space. They cost an arm and a leg. Insurance isn't cheap either. And think about having a car with no garage in this Alaska weather. Know what I mean?"

"I do."

"And I grew up in New York. We never needed them. Driving through midtown Manhattan—that will make you afraid of cars forever."

"I'm a New Yorker too, so you don't need to tell me," Ms. Torres laughed. "I can't even get in a cab without reminding myself I have life insurance."

"I know Ken loves cars, and I know what he thinks he wants to do," Ellen said. She put her arm over her son. "You're right, Ms. Torres. I should let Ken get his license."

Ken almost shrieked with happiness. It was finally happening! He hugged his mother. Then he hugged Ms. Torres.

"So what happens now?" Ellen asked.

"In order to take the license test, he has to pass my class. We start another one in the spring."

That would be a few months. Too long, Ken thought.

"There is another way," Ms. Torres said. "Since Ken already knows everything I can possibly teach him, he can take his final now. That means he has to pass a written exam, and then he has to start practicing on the road."

"Let's start now!" Ken blurted.

"One more thing, Ken. I can't pass you

unless you complete thirty hours of practice driving, in a car, with an adult. That's all there is. What do you think?"

Just then, Patty walked through the front door, carrying groceries.

"Look, an adult," Ken said.

"What are you looking at me for?" Patty asked.

"Hey, Sis, how about a big, big favor?"

✳ ✳ ✳

Meanwhile, Edmond Tremonte was still building something. It barely fit inside the garage. Its gigantic engine roared with noise. The object was covered in black paint, the same tint as its windows. With a burst of smoke, it lurched forward.

Tremonte sat inside the machine. It still needed work before he could release it. First, he needed a name for this mobile engine of destruction. He went to a storage closet and got a bucket of white paint. With a brush, he painted on the side of the machine.

MURDOZER, Edmond Tremonte wrote, in big block letters.

CHAPTER SEVEN

Ken was determined to get his license as soon as possible. He was so excited, he even woke up early to take the written portion of the exam before school. Ms. Torres was usually at school by 6:00 a.m. On Tuesday, Ken was there at 5:30. Ms. Torres found him sitting at his desk, pencil ready.

She handed him the test. "Good luck," she said.

But Ken was already scribbling answers. Everything he knew about cars and driving was finally going to matter. And he knew *everything.* Thirty minutes later, he was done.

Ms. Torres had never seen a test completed that fast. She graded it and handed it back to Ken.

"Ninety-nine percent," she said as he looked at the score. "Just short of an A+."

"Ninety-nine? What did I get wrong?"

"The question about hitting a patch of ice. You turn into the skid, not away from the skid."

"Huh. I should know that."

"You sure should! Now that you've passed, are you ready for the road?"

"Yeah," said Ken. "I'm ready to burn that baby beneath my treads."

"Thirty hours and counting." Ms. Torres pointed to her watch.

※ ※ ※

Ken had calculated the fastest way to finish thirty hours of driving. It was Tuesday, and Ken knew that the DMV was only open on weekdays. He made his plans during lunch while Benno and Stacey listened.

"School is six hours every day. That's twenty-four hours total marked off by Friday. Subtract that by the total hours from now until then."

Stacey and Benno both silently did the math.

"Fifty hours!" Stacey said.

"Wait, fifty hours!" Benno added. "I was going to say that."

"Right. Fifty hours from 3:00 p.m. today until 5:00 p.m. Friday."

"And you need to drive thirty hours."

"And have the hours signed off by Ms. Torres."

It didn't take Stacey long to figure out the problem. "When will you have time to sleep or eat or study?"

"I'll do my homework at school. I can eat on the go. And five hours of sleep a night— that will be enough."

"Five hours of sleep a night times four equals twenty. You have zero time to do anything else," Benno realized.

"It's okay, Benno. I'll wake up and drive

before school, drive after school, and drive until bed."

"But no adult is going to sit in a car for this long, right?"

"My sister Patty will. If she gets sleepy, my mom might help."

"Wow, Ken Genie, you have it figured out," Stacey said.

✳ ✳ ✳

Patty was ready to pick up Ken in the school parking lot at 3:00 p.m. exactly.

"Remind me why I'm doing this, brother?" she asked as she got out of the Eclipse. "I'm taking a sick day from work."

"Because you're my sister, and you always help me when I need it."

"While you are my brother, yet you cause me nothing but grief." She opened the driver door for him. "Now get behind the wheel."

Ken climbed into the driver seat and closed the door. Patty put something metal in his hand. "The keys, from mom."

Ken felt the texture of his Recaro seat. He gripped the steering wheel. He was born to drive this car. And he still didn't know where it had come from.

"No time to waste," Ken said. He put the key in the ignition.

The engine came to life with a perfect sound. Ken inhaled the scent of upholstery mixed with car fumes. It smelled like a new home.

"Okay, Ken, you're starting out, so remember to ease on the clutch, accelerate slowly, and then shift gears."

Ken turned to his sister and put his hand on her shoulder. "Patty, don't worry. I got this."

Ken drove for the first time. The Eclipse backed out of the parking lot and onto the road. Students leaving school gazed at him as he drove by. Suddenly, everyone was talking about Ken Genie.

For the next two days, Ken was either at school or behind the wheel. Though he obeyed traffic laws, he had never felt so free. Patty stayed in the passenger's seat and said nothing—there was nothing she could teach him. They drove through the entire town of Connor, then through the outskirts. Ken was equally amazing driving on gravel, on ice, or in a traffic jam. Nothing fazed him, and he never made a mistake. He drove from three to nine every night, then woke up at 4 a.m. to drive until school. Before long, Ken's Eclipse was a regular neighborhood sight.

Ken's nonstop driving left Benno without much to do. He decided to take a walk down Main Street. As he passed the Spiff Tube, he heard a voice from inside.

"Hey kid. You want fifty dollars?"

Fifty dollars was a lot of money for Benno. He saw Edmond Tremonte standing by a doorway to his garage. Tremonte had a huge beard now. His clothes were unwashed. His eyes were red. He smelled terrible too.

"Fifty dollars to open a garage door. All right?"

Benno agreed, and together they went inside the shop.

"Take a look at my masterpiece," Tremonte said.

Benno couldn't believe what he was looking at inside the Spiff Tube. It had treads instead of wheels and a huge front-end loader to move wreckage out of the way. Just like a bulldozer. It was covered in concrete and steel, at least a foot of each. On the side, in big block letters, was the word *MURDOZER*.

"This is my Murdozer," Tremonte explained. "Once I get in and turn it on, I have to weld the panel underneath shut. When I'm inside, I can't get out. Unfortunately, a garage door signal doesn't work through this much steel. Open my door for me."

He put the fifty-dollar bill in Benno's hand. Then he started crawling underneath the vehicle, whistling happily.

"It has two TV monitors, so I can see outside without windows. I have enough food and spare oxygen in here to last me months, so I never have to go outside."

Benno was still amazed and a little confused.

"Best of all . . ." There was silence, and then Benno heard a loud noise like feedback. Tremonte's voice was amplified through two gigantic speakers on the outside of the vehicle. "I INSTALLED A LOUDSPEAKER, SO EVERYONE WILL KNOW IT IS ME, EDMOND TREMONTE, WHO SEEKS REVENGE TODAY. NOW, OPEN THE DOOR PLEASE." His voice crackled through the speakers. "THERE IS A SQUARE BUTTON ON THE PANEL NEXT TO THE GARAGE."

Benno pressed the button and the doors opened. "Did you say revenge? Against what?"

"WHY, THE GENIES OF COURSE." The Murdozer turned on and slowly moved out of the garage. It turned left on Main Street and rolled westward.

The Genies? Benno realized he made a major mistake.

CHAPTER EIGHT

Finally, it was Friday. Ellen woke Ken with a surprise.

"I called school. You're sick today," she said. "Let's knock out a few extra hours to give Patty a break."

Ken was only too happy to drive with his mom. He had eleven hours left to get his license.

After freeing the Murdozer, Edmond Tremonte slept in its belly until the next morning. Once dawn came, he opened a parcel of food from a refrigerator under the dashboard and then started the vehicle. He turned on the two traffic cameras. One was in front of the vehicle. One was in back. The Murdozer would be slow and very noisy. Tremonte pressed the button on his loudspeaker as he munched on a sandwich.

"ATTENTION, CONNOR. THIS IS EDMOND TREMONTE, THE RICHEST MAN YOU KNOW. PLEASE GO ABOUT YOUR DAILY BUSINESS AND IGNORE THIS GLORIOUS VEHICLE."

"Now, to visit the Genies," Tremonte said to himself. If Edmond Tremonte couldn't have his car back, he was going to make sure that nobody used it.

The dozer barely went thirty MPH. Citizens of Connor started to notice a crazy tank in the center of town.

Tremonte parked by the Genie house and turned on the loudspeaker again. "ATTENTION, GENIE FAMILY. ONE MORE WARNING. PLEASE RETURN

MY PROPERTY."

Patty was at work, and Ken and Ellen were off driving. The car was gone.

Where did they go? he thought.

Connor was such a small town that there was no DMV. The nearest location was forty-five minutes away, in a bigger city called Farber.

"How many hours do you have left?" Ellen asked as they drove toward the city.

"Seven. I can finish them off once we're in Farber."

After first period that day, Stacey grabbed some books out of her locker. She had missed Ken in I-Tech class. She noticed Benno passing by.

"Have you seen Ken at all today?" Benno asked.

"Ms. Torres said he was sick," Stacey said.

"On the day he gets his license?"

Stacey thought for a second. "Maybe he's not sick."

"Something weird happened last night," Benno said nervously. He was about to tell her about what he saw at the Spiff Tube, when a voice came over the intercom.

"ATTENTION, STUDENTS," the principal said. "THIS IS AN EMERGENCY. WE'RE GETTING WORD FROM POLICE THAT... SOME SORT OF MONSTER CAR MIGHT BE HEADED TO THIS SCHOOL! PLEASE FOLLOW STANDARD FIRE DRILL RULES."

"Monster car?" Stacey asked.

"A Murderdozer," Benno recalled. "We need to find Ken and his family. Now."

"I'll drive," Stacey said. She grabbed her keys from her locker and closed it. She and Benno went out the back way, toward her vehicle.

Edmond Tremonte had decided to demolish some public buildings. First, he went to the local police station and smashed it to bits, burying the department in wreckage. Then he drove his Murdozer through the walls of the fire station.

Police appeared and began firing on the vehicle. It was completely bulletproof. Next, the police set up a barricade to prevent traffic from coming through. The dozer busted through that as well. Authorities climbed on it, bashed it, but nothing could stop it. Tremonte was an unstoppable destructive force. He wrecked everything his cameras could see.

"BRING ME THE MITSUBISHI," he kept saying. "OR I WILL BURN THIS TOWN TO THE GROUND."

As they left school, Stacey and Benno could see wreckage in the distance. Other cars were driving as fast as they could in the opposite direction of the Murdozer.

Suddenly, a Corolla swerved into the path of the Murdozer as it turned another corner. Someone got out—Ms. Torres.

She waved to get Tremonte's attention. "Stop! Why are you doing this?"

"AS LONG AS THERE IS NO MITSUBISHI, I WILL NOT STOP. THE POLICE CANNOT STOP ME. YOU CANNOT STOP ME. ONLY KEN GENIE CAN STOP THIS. NOW MOVE OUT OF MY WAY."

"No," said Ms. Torres.

"THEN SAY GOODBYE TO YOUR CAR." He rammed into Ms. Torres's Corolla at full speed. She jumped out of the way just in time. The car split into strips of scrap metal.

"Tremonte, you've gone too far!" yelled a police officer. He turned to his fellow officers. "Men, I think we need to find Ken Genie and his car."

Ken was in Farber, driving over smooth city streets. He had sixty minutes to go until he finished his thirty hours. He turned into the DMV parking lot. For the next hour, he spun in circles around the lot. It might have been the longest hour of his life.

But at 4:00 p.m., Ken and Ellen exited the vehicle and walked into the DMV. A special bulletin lit up the TV inside.

"We are receiving word that the town of Connor, Alaska, is under attack," the broadcaster said. "A local businessman has created a devastating vehicle of destruction."

They showed a clip of the police station falling apart. Rubble was everywhere, and you could hear screaming. Ken's mouth was wide open. So was Ellen's.

The broadcaster continued. "The man claims he wants a car that belongs to him. A customized Mitsubishi Eclipse. He says he will not stop the destruction until the car is his."

"We have to go back," Ken said.

"What about your license?" his mom replied.

"He might hurt someone. If the car is all he wants, I need to give it to him."

They left just as someone called Ken's name for the license test.

✳ ✳ ✳

Ken drove home at top speed. By the time he and his mom were back in Connor, blocks of houses were being swept away, and the police were still trying to stop it. Officers set controlled explosions, but nothing could pierce the dozer's shell.

Ken sped toward the carnage. A policewoman saw him from afar: "There it is!"

The police blockade moved so Ken could drive through. Now he was only feet away from the Murdozer. It towered over his Mitsubishi.

Ken got out of the car and held up his hands. His mother did the same.

"I THOUGHT YOU WOULDN'T BE BACK, KEN GENIE."

"Here I am. And here's my car. Take it,

and stop hurting my town." He held up the keys.

"NO, NO. YOU HAD YOUR CHANCE. NOW I AM STUCK IN THIS MACHINE. I DON'T WANT TO TAKE YOUR VEHICLE ANYMORE . . ." The Murdozer moved forward. "I WANT TO CRUSH IT INTO SCRAP UNDER MY TREADS."

The Murdozer accelerated toward the Eclipse. The dozer moved slowly, but Ken had no time to get back in the car and move it to safety.

"Run, Mom!" he yelled. But Ellen did not move.

Tremonte inched closer. "HERE I COME. YOUR FAMILY HAS MADE ME SUFFER. NOW I PAY IT BACK."

Ken stood loyally by his vehicle. Ellen stood loyally by her son. It looked like the end for both of them.

Then came the sound of another engine coming closer. At top speed, a beat-up Oldsmobile pulled around the blockade and charged headlong into the side of the

Murdozer. Before the crash, a person jumped out of the car's seat. He hit the pavement hard. Ken and Ellen ducked behind the Eclipse to hide from the shower of metal and sparks.

The Oldsmobile was demolished, but it had pushed the dozer off the road slightly. The Mitsubishi had time to get away.

Ken adjusted his glasses and then recognized the driver on the ground. It was Cliff.

CHAPTER NINE

All of Ken's memories of Cliff came back in an instant. The talks, the car rides, the days spent hanging out . . .

Unfortunately, there was no time to reconnect. The Murdozer was still working.

"Hello, Ken," Cliff said. "Hey mom."

"Hello, Cliff." Any anger Ellen felt toward her oldest was now gone. She was just relieved to see her other son.

"Give me your keys," Cliff said. "We're backing out now."

The Murdozer turned to face them.

"CLIFF GENIE? YOU ARE FINALLY MINE."

Ken handed his brother the keys. "Why can't I drive?" he asked.

"Do you have your license?" Cliff responded.

"Well, er . . . it's a long story."

"I have a story too," Cliff said. "Get in the car. Not you, Mom. You should go to the police and try to come up with a new plan. In case ours doesn't work."

"Can you keep Ken safe?" Ellen asked.

"I made a promise. To Dad."

That was good enough for Ellen Genie. She kissed Cliff and ran back through the police blockade. Now it was just the brothers.

Cliff got in the driver's seat. Ken got in the passenger's seat.

"IF I CANNOT CRUSH THIS CAR, I WILL CRUSH THIS TOWN."

"Let's move," Cliff said. He turned on the ignition, spun 180 degrees, and headed out of town again. "We're going into the country for a minute."

Soon they were off pavement and on a gravel road. Connor was behind them once more.

"It's good that that thing is so slow," Cliff said, as he parked off on a side road. "I have a plan, but first you probably need a big question answered."

"Now?" Ken asked, anxiously. "He's still coming for us. That thing is slow, but we can't really hide when he destroys everything in his path."

"I know he's coming. And this is very important."

"What is it?"

"I put the Mitsubishi Eclipse in your driveway."

Ken was shocked. "Why?"

"Dad told me to."

"But Dad is dead."

"Let me back up for a second." Cliff told him the whole story.

Many years ago, Del Genie was working late at the Spiff Tube. At the end of his shift, a man walked in, covered with snow. He had been driving his new car until a massive storm hit. The man had pulled over in the middle of the road and stopped the vehicle. Then the car wouldn't turn back on. He had walked more than a mile to find shelter and barely made it to the Spiff Tube.

"I will find your car and bring it back," Del Genie promised. He trekked through the snowstorm to find the man's ride. Del dug the snow from under the wheels, then put the car in neutral. He pushed it a whole mile, back the way he came. It took him three hours.

Then he fixed the man's car, like he always did. Del had that gift.

The man was so happy that he made a generous decision. "I'd like you to have my car," he said. "It's a Mitsubishi Eclipse with a custom turbocharged engine." After all, Del had saved the car and maybe the man's life.

Del said that he didn't need it. But Del's

boss, Edmond Tremonte, overheard what was happening.

"I'm afraid it is company policy that we cannot accept gifts to employees," Tremonte said. "Of course, if you want to donate it to the shop . . ."

"I want him to have it," the man said. "He worked for it. He deserves it." He even signed over his registration papers.

Tremonte tried to patiently explain that this was illegal, but the man refused to budge. Del wasn't sure what to do.

"Give me a dollar," the man said to Del.

Del gave the man a dollar from his coat pocket.

"You just bought my car. You mind driving me to a hotel?"

Del was speechless.

The next day, the man was gone, but the car was still there. Del still had the keys. The car's papers were in his name.

The next day at work, Edmond needled his employee. "Did he really give you the car?"

"No," Del lied. He had hidden it in a

storage garage another town over. "He took it and left."

"Really?"

"Really." Del hated to lie, but he knew what he wanted for the car. He wanted to give it to his youngest son.

He told no one until his last conversation with Cliff. On his deathbed, he explained that there was a secret car for Ken, and it would be delivered when Ken turned sixteen. Del made Cliff promise that he would protect his family and that he would deliver the car himself.

Eight years later, Cliff honored his father's request.

※ ※ ※

"I've been staying in Farber ever since," Cliff concluded. "I heard your name on the news and raced down here."

Ken had many more questions. Why did Cliff leave so long ago? Why did he never call? But the Murdozer was still looking for them. At least Ken had his brother back.

Suddenly, the brothers heard the ring of a familiar loudspeaker. "YOU BOYS CANNOT HIDE FROM ME HERE. I WILL FLATTEN ALL THE TREES IN MY WAY."

The dozer was behind them again, getting closer. Cliff gunned the ignition and raced away. But the road came to a dead end. There was nowhere to turn—except forward onto a frozen lake. It was the lake where Ken had daydreamed days earlier.

"BETTER RUN, BOYS." The Murdozer was as wide as the street. There was no way to move around it.

"Cliff, maybe we should get out and leave this thing behind."

"Never," Cliff said. "This car is yours. I promised Dad I would protect it. And you. Maybe I didn't step up for my family before, but I will now."

Cliff and Ken sat in the car together and braced for impact. Cliff grabbed Ken's right hand and squeezed.

"I'm sorry for leaving you and Mom and

Patty behind," he said.

"It's okay, Cliff. You came back," Ken replied.

The Murdozer was only a dozen feet away.

Suddenly, the dozer stopped. It started jerking back and forth.

"MY CAMERA. WHERE DID MY CAMERA GO?"

On top of the Murdozer's concrete shell, Ken could see Benno and Stacey. They had scaled the dozer and were riding on top.

"Break the cameras!" Stacey yelled from above. "He can't see!"

Benno smashed a camera on the front of the vehicle. Tremonte was blind.

"WHAT HAVE YOU DONE?"

"Time to move, guys!" Benno yelled, still riding the dozer. The police had surrounded the area. Benno and Stacey jumped off the rear bumper and ran behind a new blockade.

Tremonte started laughing. "I DON'T NEED EYES. I ONLY NEED TO GO FORWARD. THERE'S STILL NOWHERE TO HIDE, GENIES."

The Murdozer could not be stopped. Cliff looked out to the frozen lake.

"Hey, Ken," he said. "You know a lot about cars. On ice, do I turn into the skid or away from the skid?"

"Into the skid," Ken replied.

"Good to know," Cliff said. He accelerated forward, kicking up snow where the street ended.

Past a layer of trees, Cliff drove the car over a ravine. The Mitsubishi crashed onto the icy lake below. The ice did not break.

"Woo-hoo!" Cliff cried. The tires squealed against the ice. Ken could hear it start to crack.

The dozer kept coming forward, past the layer of trees.

"WHERE ARE YOU?" he asked. "WHERE IS THE SOUND OF BREAKING MET..."

The Murdozer dropped front-first into the lake. Ice cracked, and water flowed up from the hole forming underneath the vehicle. Edmond Tremonte, still blind, began to sink.

"WHY AM I FALLING? WHAT IS HAPPENING?" Tremonte tried to ask.

Ken got out of the car and yelled to warn him. "You're sinking underwater! Get out now!"

"WHAT? I CAN'T LEAVE HERE. THERE'S NO DOOR."

Cliff also got out of the car. "We have to save him," Ken said to his brother.

"SAVE ME? SAVE ME? NEVER." Half the dozer was beneath the lake. "EDMOND TREMONTE GOES DOWN WITH HIS KILLSHIP."

It sank farther and farther downward. "THE JOKE IS ON YOU, GENIES. MY MURDOZER IS WATERPROOF. I HAVE ENOUGH FOOD, WATER, AND OXYGEN TO LAST FOR MONTHS. I CAN STAY DOWN HERE AS LONG AS I WANT. IF CONNOR WON'T HAVE ME, THE BOTTOM OF THIS LAKE WILL BE MY NEW HO . . ."

The loudspeaker fizzed out underwater. Tremonte was silent. He sank to the bottom, trapped in the belly of his machine.

Ken and Cliff sat on the hood of the Mitsubishi and watched the Murdozer disappear. Was it really possible for a man to live underwater, in a giant waterproof mobile fortress? It seemed crazy. But Edmond Tremonte was gone.

CHAPTER TEN

The authorities took a long time to figure out what happened that day. The town of Connor had never seen such destruction. It would take time to rebuild.

Ken asked an officer if it was possible for Edmond Tremonte to still be alive at the bottom of the lake.

"It's too cold down there," the man said, "and there's no way we can open a death trap like that while it's underwater. We may have to camp out here and wait to arrest him when he comes up for air."

The Murdozer had shaken the ice floes in the lake. To retrieve the Mitsubishi, the police had to tow it with steel cables.

Ken's car was safe.

Ellen and Patty came to greet them. Ken didn't know what his sister would say, seeing Cliff after so many years.

She gave him a bear hug. Then Ellen did the same. For a while, no one said a word.

"I'm sorry, Mom," Cliff said. "For so much."

"You can tell me how sorry you are over dinner."

Patty spoke up. "Are you staying for good?"

"Should I?" Cliff said.

As the police continued investigating the crime scene, Stacey and Benno joined them.

"You saved us!" Ken said.

"We had been looking for you all day, Ken!" Stacey said. "We drove everywhere. It was easy, once we started following this guy."

"We sneaked behind the dozer and climbed on top," Benno said. "It was Stacey's idea to take the cameras away. I had the same idea, but she said it first."

"You're pretty smart," Ken said to Stacey. She beamed. Coming from car genius Ken Genie, that was a serious compliment.

"What happens to Connor now?" Benno said.

"We'll rebuild," Ken said. "But first, I need to have dinner with my family."

"See you at school on Monday?" Stacey asked.

"Yeah, you'll see me. You'll see me behind the wheel."

＊ ＊ ＊

It was a miracle. The Genie family house was still standing, and the family was back together. All the anger Ellen and Patty felt toward Cliff was gone. They wanted him to come back.

"I can't stay," Cliff explained, as he sat with his family at the dinner table. Between stays in Farber, he had been working in fisheries all over Canada, and he needed to return to work. Ken was not happy to hear this. After what they had been through, he could not believe Cliff would leave.

After dinner, Ellen visited Ken's room.

"Want to talk?" she asked.

"I can't believe Cliff is ditching us again. You were right, Mom."

"Right about what?"

"He always leaves us behind when we need him."

Ellen sat on the bed next to Ken. "But I wasn't right, Ken. I let him down too. But that's what families do sometimes. Your brother made mistakes. I made mistakes. But we still hold onto each other, no matter what."

"No matter what," Ken repeated. "But it's not fair that he gets to leave again, and I'm still stuck in this town."

Ellen knew it was time to offer her son a chance to spread his wings.

"School will be out for break in a week. Why don't you go with him?"

"What do you mean?"

"Cliff needs a car, and you need to get out of town. How about you take a trip together?"

Cliff was suddenly excited. "A road trip?"

"That's right."

"Sounds good, Mom, except for one thing."

"What's that?"

"I still need a license."

✳ ✳ ✳

The next week, two brothers in a Mitsubishi Eclipse crossed the Canadian border. The windows were open, and a strong cold breeze blew inside. They sat together, talking. They talked about their lives, their loves, their goals in life.

Ken was driving. Cliff was in the passenger's seat. They cruised along a freeway that never seemed to end. Del would have been proud to see them.

How can life get any better? Ken thought. He was on an adventure with the greatest brother in the world. The future seemed to unfold in front of them. The future was the open road. Ken adjusted his glasses, the better to see their journey ahead.

THE MITSUBISHI ECLIPSE

MODEL HISTORY

Mitsubishi began in Japan in 1870 as a shipping business. Eventually, it got into shipbuilding. It created some of the biggest ocean vessels of the time. After World War II (1939–1945), the company split up into smaller parts. In 1969 the Mitsubishi Motors Corporation was formed. It focused strictly on cars. Mitsubishi released four generations of the Eclipse between 1989 and 2011.

The original Eclipse was a sporty car powered by a four-cylinder engine. Its front-wheel drive gave the Eclipse superior traction, especially in wet or slippery conditions, and better stability. For those who wished for a more powerful engine, the Eclipse GS Turbo featured a turbocharged engine while the Eclipse GSX included the turbocharged engine as well as all-wheel drive (AWD). In 1996 the first convertible model of the Eclipse was released, the Spyder.

With the 2000 model, Mitsubishi did away with the Eclipse's all-wheel drive and turbocharged engines. The new Eclipse came in five-speed manual or four-speed automatic transmission. The fourth-generation Mitsubishi Eclipse (2005–2011) saw another increase in horsepower.

THE MITSUBISHI EVO

The Mitsubishi Lancer Evolution, better known as the Evo, is a high-performance sedan that has four-wheel drive and a two-liter turbocharged engine. Like the Eclipse, the Evo is popular among racers. Mitsubishi tested similar vehicles throughout the 1980s. In 1992 the Lancer Evolution I came on the scene. The first model borrowed its turbocharged engine and four-wheel drive from an earlier model, the Galant VR-4.

At first, Mitsubishi made twenty-five thousand of the Lancer Evo. Within three days, all twenty-five thousand cars were sold out. So Mitsubishi built 2,500 more, and then they sold out. There were two versions of the first Lancer Evolution: the RS (or Racing Sport) version and the GSR (Grand Sport Racing) version. The RS was made for racing only, so it did not have as many features as the other car. Mitsubishi did not design imports for a non-Japanese audience until the beginning of 1999, with the Lancer Evolution VI. In 2003 the Lancer Evolution VIII arrived on American shores. Since

2003 only two new models of the Lancer Evo have been developed: the Evo IX, in 2005, and the Evo X, in 2007.

THE MITSUBISHI ECLIPSE ON FILM

In pop culture, the Mitsubishi Eclipse is known for its appearance in *The Fast and the Furious*. LAPD officer Brian O'Connor used the 1995 Mitsubishi Eclipse RS in races at the start of the first film in the series. The car in the film had a horsepower of 210 and a 2-liter 4-cylinder engine.

THE ECLIPSE TODAY

The 2012 Eclipse car had a sporty, sleek design. However, the car did not do well sales-wise, which forced Mitsubishi to take the model off the market in 2012, ending a twenty-three-year streak as one of the world's highest-performing compact sports cars.

KEN'S MITSUBISHI ECLIPSE

ENGINE: turbo model 4G63 customized engine, front wheel drive, 2.0 liter, 210 horsepower at 6,000 RPM; five-speed manual transmission; installed cold-air intake system and hard intercooler pipes; upgraded exhaust system with new turbo downpipe and blowoff valve (reduces pressure exerted on the engine) and double tipped stainless steel exhaust; performance spark plugs and wires; replaced air filters (these remove dust particles from the air); installed underdrive pulley (this reduce drag on the engine and amp up the horsepower); installed oil pressure and oil temperature gauges, and air/fuel ratio gauge

DRIVETRAIN: custom throttle linkage; adjust the clutch and top off clutch fluid; transverse-mounted 4 cylinder, 16 valve DOHC (double overhead camshaft), iron blocks with aluminum cylinder heads

SUSPENSION: new front and rear sway bars; installed new tower bars; replace struts with adjustable ones and replace shocks (even

though the Eclipse hasn't been driven much,
it's been around a long time so it's important
to update parts like these that may have been
worn by weather and age)

BRAKES: installed new front and rear brake
pads; four-wheel drive ABS (anti-lock braking
system); performance rotor kit

WHEELS/TIRES: larger tires and 16" Alloy 5
spoke wheels; installed rims (for better
performance—and they look awesome)

EXTERIOR: two door hatchback; weatherproof
tarp cover; installed projector headlights;
high-rise spoiler; hood scoop on the front; hood
pins

INTERIOR: black leather interior; Recaro seats;
needle calibration on gauge faces; floor mats;
new steering wheel; new shift knob

ELECTRONICS: new speaker system; installed
manual boost controller; flywheel; install fuel
injector; automatic boost gauge

Check out the rest of the
TURBOCHARGED series:

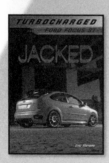